My dear mouse friends,

Have I ever told you how much I love science fiction? I've always wanted to write incredible adventures set in another dimension, but I've never believed that parallel universes exist . . . until now!

That's because my good friend Professor Paws von Volt, the brilliant, secretive scientist, has just made an incredible discovery. Thanks to some mousetropic calculations, he determined that there are many different dimensions in time and space, where anything could be possible.

The professor's work inspired me to write this science fiction adventure in which my family and I travel through space in search of new worlds. We're a fabumouse crew: the spacemice!

I hope you enjoy this intergalactic adventure!

Geronimo Stilton

PROFESSOR PAWS VON VOLT

THE SPACEMICE

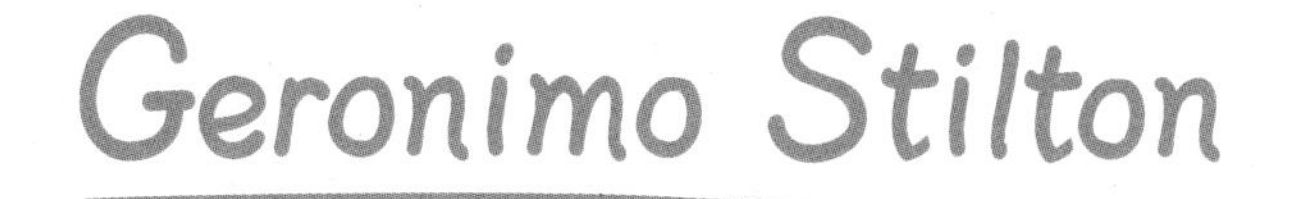

ICE PLANET ADVENTURE

Scholastic Inc.

ISBN 978-0-545-74619-9

Based on an original idea by Elisabetta Dami.

www.geronimostilton.com

Published by Scholastic Inc., 557 Broadway, New York, NY 10012.

Text by Geronimo Stilton
Original title *L'invasione dei dispettosi Ponf Ponf*
Cover by Flavio Ferron
Interior illustrations by Giuseppe Facciotto (design) and Daniele Verzini (color)
Graphics by Chiara Cebraro

Special thanks to AnnMarie Anderson
Translated by Lidia Morson Tramontozzi
Interior design by Kevin Callahan / BNGO Books

12 11 10 9 8 7 6 17 18 19 20/0

Printed in the U.S.A. 40
First printing, February 2015

In the darkness of the farthest galaxy in time and space is a spaceship inhabited exclusively by mice.

This fabumouse vessel is called the **MouseStar 1**, *and I am its captain!*

I am Geronimo Stiltonix, a somewhat accident-prone mouse who (to tell you the truth) would rather be writing novels than steering a spaceship.

But for now, my adventurous family and I are busy traveling around the universe on exciting intergalactic missions.

THIS IS THE LATEST ADVENTURE OF THE SPACEMICE!

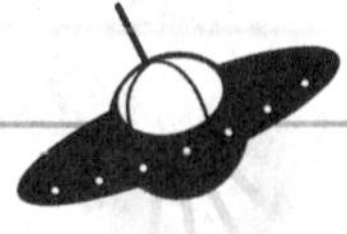

The Captain Never Gets a Day Off!

It all began on a QUIET Friday afternoon. The week was almost over, and I couldn't wait to leave the CONTROL ROOM'S headquarters and get back to my cabin. I was exhausted! Why? It had been a tough week! What am I saying? It had been a very tough week! No, a terribly tough week!

I had rescued two lost spaceships, defended the crew from alien werewolves, tested a new interstellar spacesuit, and attended the ribbon-cutting ceremony for a new intergalactic art mouseum.

In other words, I had been very, very busy!

Why, oh why does everyone always expect so much from me? Could it be because I'm the captain?

Oh, excuse me! I almost forgot to introduce myself. My name is Stiltonix, Geronimo Stiltonix. I'm the captain of MOUSESTAR 1, the most mousetropic SPACESHIP in the far-off Cheddar Galaxy. But truth be told, my real dream has always been to be a WRITER! I have been wanting to write a novel about the adventures of the spacemice for years, but I can't seem to find the time. There's always a PROBLEM on the *MouseStar 1* that needs to be fixed.

But let's get back to that QUIET Friday afternoon. The weekend was about to start and I had big plans for my Saturday, which was my day off!

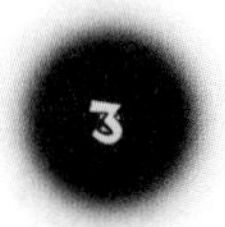

I planned to:

1. Get up late and eat breakfast in bed, lazily munching on a creamy Gorgonzola muffin.
2. Put on my comfortable and practical casual uniform.
3. Get my whiskers trimmed at **BRUSH**, the trendiest barbershop on the entire spaceship.

Do Not Disturb

As soon as I got to my cabin, I hung this **SIGN** on my door. It wasn't exactly the truth, as I intended to spend the evening **snoring** instead of *working*! But everyone knows a good rest is very important. So, I slipped into my pajamas, turned on my favorite CD, *Relaxing Music for the Busy Mouse*, and sank into bed.

Please do not disturb.
The captain is working!

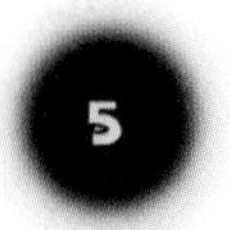

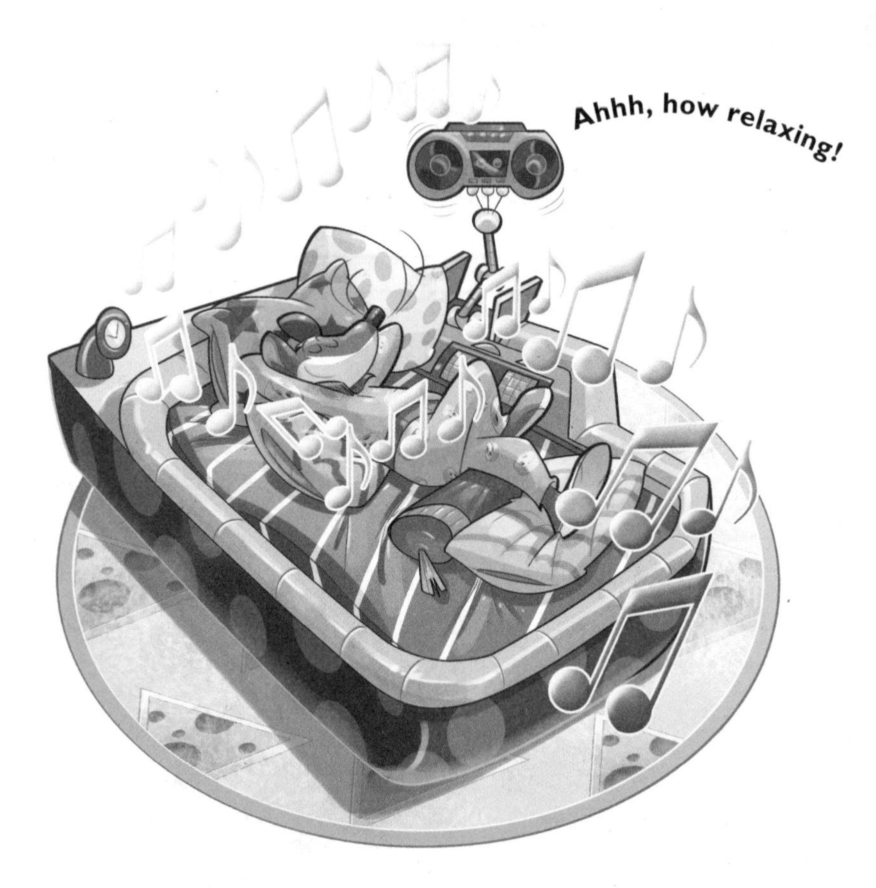

I slept almost until morning. I would have slept even longer, but suddenly . . .

BEEP! BEEEEP! BEEEEEP!

It was coming from my wrist phone!

Still half-asleep, I tried to turn **OFF** the

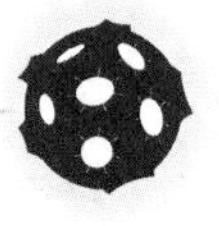

alarm, but instead, I pushed the ON button! What a mistake! My wrist phone came to life.

"Geronimo!" a voice bellowed. "Wake up! I bet you're still SNORING like a Plutonian sloth! But not for long—I'll straighten you out!"

I would have recognized that voice among a thousand, no, ten thousand, no, ten million voices. It was my grandfather, William Stiltonix! He didn't even give me a chance to respond before he began bombarding me with orders.

"Hurry up and get dressed. I'll be there to pick you up in two astroseconds! They're waiting for us at the space tennis center!"

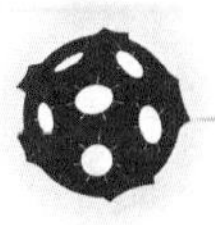

I looked at the clock: It was FOUR in the morning! I tried to OBJECT.

"But Grandfather, it's really EARLY!" I squeaked. "What are we going to do at the tennis center at this hour? And who's waiting for us?"

"I can't believe you forgot!" Grandfather William roared. "Today is the FINAL match in the INTERGALACTIC TENNIS TOURNAMENT!"

"Ahem, er, sorry, Grandfather," I replied. "You know I don't care much for sports. I prefer to read and write science fiction."

My grandfather glared at me with disapproval from the wrist phone video monitor.

"Then you probably don't know that I, Admiral William Stiltonix, your grandfather,

will be COMPETING in the tournament!" he squeaked indignantly. "But I have a problem: Yesterday, my tennis partner slipped on an interstellar banana peel and sprained an ankle. That's why I'm picking you up. You'll be subbing for him!"

I felt a chill run down my tail. Play space tennis with Grandfather William? What a nightmare! Grandfather is very, very competitive. He hates to lose! I tried to dissuade him.

"Grandfather, you know I stink at tennis—" I began, but he cut me off.

"Of course I know that!" he replied. "That's why I'm coming now to pick you up. ASTRO AGASSI, the greatest tennis master of all time, is waiting for us at the court. He'll **TEACH** you for five straight hours. By the time the tournament begins at ten, you'll be ready!"

I WANTED TO CRY. Five straight hours of lessons! And then I would have to play in the tennis finals with my grandfather! I was **TIRED** just thinking about it. I tried a second time to get my grandfather to understand what a terrible idea this was.

"But Grandfather, er, today is actually my **DAY OFF**!"

Unfortunately, changing my grandfather's mind is as hard as trying to get a **meteorite** to deviate from its path.

"Day off?" my grandfather SCOFFED. "The captain never gets a DAY OFF. Now, come on! You'll see how much you'll love playing tennis! There's no BETTER way to stay in shape. You should thank me for offering you this unique opportunity!"

A second later, he abruptly hung up.

I sighed. It was no use. I would have to play in the competition. I opened my automatic closet and squeaked out an order: "Gear for SPACE TENNIS, please!"

From the Encyclopedia Galactica

SPACE TENNIS

Space tennis is played with a racquet and a small ball. It would be just like regular tennis except that there's no gravity in space. Without gravity, it's almost impossible to hit the ball!

Captain, You Must Come at Once!

An ASTROMINUTE later, I was dressed to the nines. I was about to leave my cabin when my wrist phone went off.

BeeP! BeeeP! BeeeeP!

It was Professor Greenfur, the resident scientist on the MOUSESTAR 1. Why would he be calling me at four o'clock in the morning? Were we under attack from STINKING alien monsters? Or had an epidemic of Martian measles broken out on the ship? Or perhaps there was a serious PROBLEM in the greenhouse?

"What is it, Professor Greenfur?"

I replied immediately. "Is there an emergency?"

I was almost hoping there was an EMERGENCY, because it would mean I wouldn't have to play in the **tournament** with my grandfather! But I was out of luck.

"No emergency, Captain," the professor replied. "But I do have a new ultragalactic invention to show you. I'd like to see you right away!"

"I'm afraid that won't be possible," I said with a sigh. "I'm on my way to *play* in the space tennis tournament with Grandfather William."

At that moment, my grandfather **burst** into my cabin.

"Aren't you ready yet, **GRANDSON**?" he squeaked at me. "Move it! Come on, let's go! Don't waste your time with that wrist phone! What would you do without me, huh? You'd waste your day **EXPLORING THE GALAXY AND COMBING COMET TAILS**! Or you'd be in the laboratory with Professor Greenfur **studying the yellow-bearded mousequito**! Or you'd be **TEXTING a THOUSAND MESSAGES TO YOUR FRIENDS FROM OTHER PLANETS**!"

I wanted to explain that I wouldn't have been doing any of those silly things—I would have been busy writing my SCIENCE FICTION novel. But he's my grandfather, and I can never say no to friends and family. He was so looking forward to that tournament . . . I couldn't leave him in the LURCH!

"I'm ready, Grandfather!" I told him. Then I turned to my wrist phone.

"I'll be by later to see your invention," I promised the professor. I hoped I could make it!

We turned to leave and my phone rang again.

BEEP! BEEEP!
BEEEEP!

My grandfather scowled.

"From now on, you have to concentrate on one thing only: the tennis match," he ordered me. "Turn off that phone — now!"

"But Grandfather, it's Benjamin!" I protested.

My grandfather's snout suddenly softened like Brie cheese. Benjamin is my **SWEET** little nephew, and my grandfather and I both have a *soft* spot for him.

"Okay, see what he wants," he told me. "But be **QUICK** about it!"

"Hi, Benjamin!" I answered. "How are you?"

"I'm fine, Uncle," he replied. "I'm sorry to call you so **EARLY** in the morning, but I know you're an early riser. Are you busy today?"

"Well, this morning I'm competing in the space tennis tournament with Grandfather," I replied. "Then I have to visit Professor Greenfur in his LAB. After that, I want to have my whiskers trimmed at the barbershop. And later on, I hope to write a chapter in my new book! Why do you ask?"

"Oh, no reason," Benjamin replied with a TINY sigh. He sounded so disappointed!

"What is it, my little CHEESE NIBLET?" I asked, concerned.

"It's nothing," he answered. "Don't worry about it!"

"But why are you so sad?" I insisted. I hated to see my nephew upset. "Do you need my help researching an ASTEROID for school? Do you have to study for a really hard quantum physics quiz?"

"No, it's not about school," he replied.

Yay! Astral Park!

"It's just that Bugsy Wugsy and I wanted to go to ASTRAL PARK, the new amousement park. But if you're busy, don't worry about it . . ."

Even though Benjamin told me not to worry about it, I could tell it meant **A LOT** to him. So I promised we'd go to **ASTRAL PARK** in the afternoon. And to think that it was supposed to have been my **DAY OFF**! But the *best*—actually, the **WORST**—was yet to come!

A Hopeless Case!

The space tennis lesson with Astro Agassi was a galactic disaster! Why? It was simple: For over five (yes, five!) hours, he tried to teach me the basic principles of space tennis. But there was NOTHING he could do. There was NOTHING anyone could do!

I WAS JUST REALLY, REALLY BAD AT SPACE TENNIS!

At the end of the lesson, a dejected Astro went over to my grandfather, shaking his head.

"Galactic Gorgonzola!" he exclaimed. "You were right, Admiral, as always. Your grandson is a hopeless case!"

I felt awful. It wasn't just because I had disappointed my grandfather. It was also because after five (yes, five!) exhausting hours of intense training, the real tennis tournament was about to start. And it could last anywhere from two or three to even five (yes, five!) MORE hours!

As you can imagine, the tournament was a real nightmare. My forehand ZIGZAGGED across the court, my backhand went backward, and my serve DIDN'T SERVE a thing!

Grandfather and I were eliminated

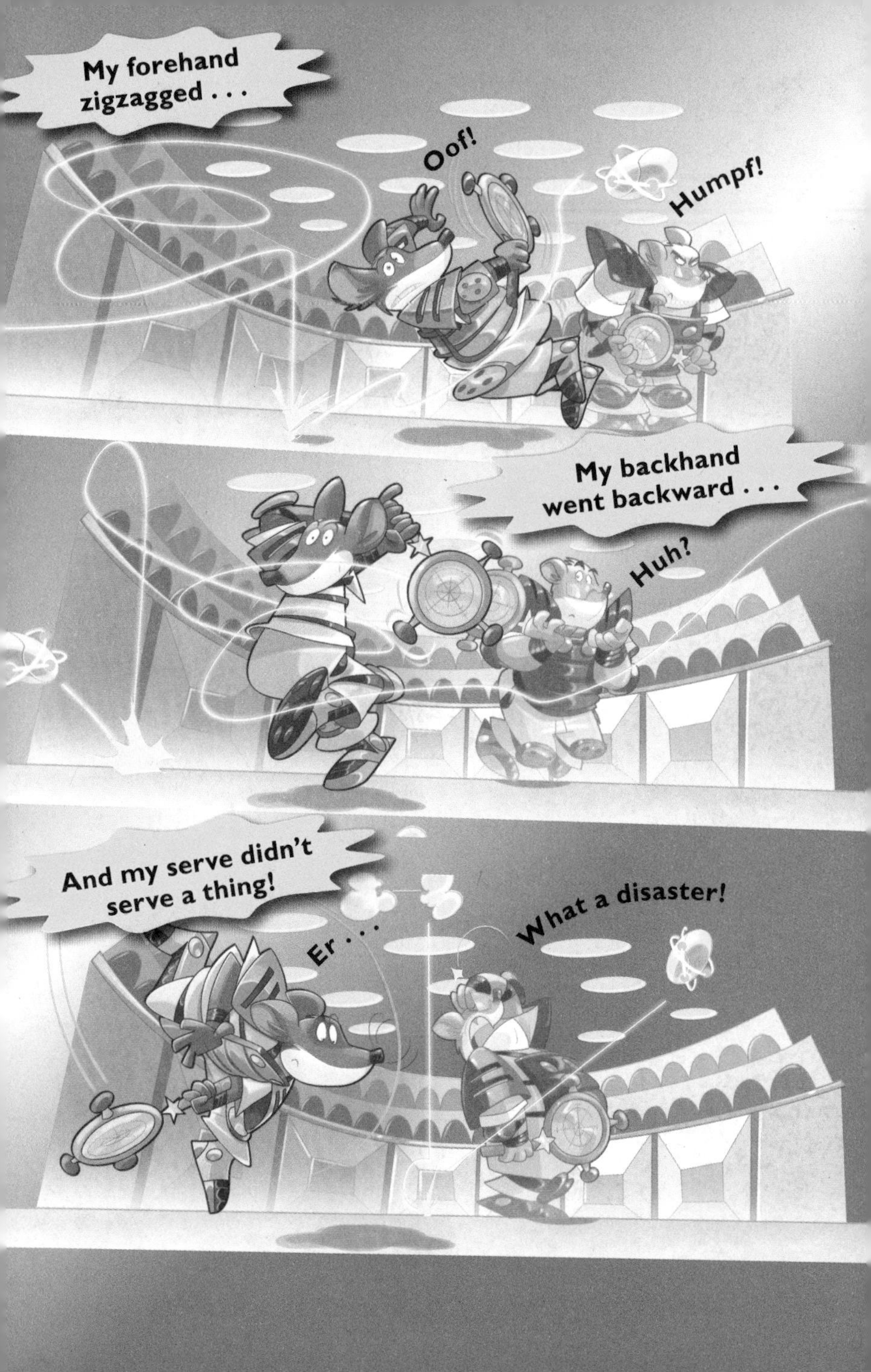
My forehand zigzagged . . .
Oof!
Humpf!
My backhand went backward . . .
Huh?
And my serve didn't serve a thing!
Er . . .
What a disaster!

in the first round. I was *mortified*. I had embarrassed my grandfather in front of all his friends at the SPACE TENNIS CLUB! I hung my head in shame. I didn't even bother following my grandfather back to the LOCKER ROOM to get my things. Instead, I snuck out of the space tennis center as fast as my paws would carry me. Still wearing my tennis shorts and sneakers, I jumped into an ASTROTAXI.

"I'd like to go to Professor Greenfur's laboratory," I told the driver. "And get there QUICKLY, please!"

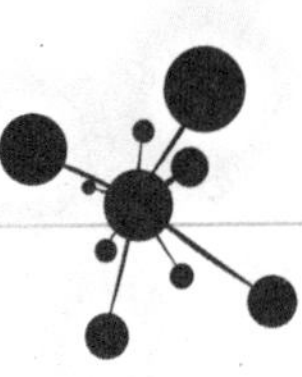

You're the Best, Uncle G!

The astrotaxi arrived at Professor Greenfur's lab in the blink of an eye. The professor showed me a strange machine that looked like a little suitcase with a handlebar and pedals attached to it.

"Here's my new invention, CAPTAIN!" he announced proudly. "It's a portable stellar energy generator. It can be dismantled in thirty seconds, it's very light, and it operates using . . . MUSCULAR ENERGY!"

Professor Greenfur hopped onto the machine and started to pedal furiously. A series of COLORED LIGHTBULBS that were suspended from the ceiling lit up.

"My creation is ideal for rodents who love ADVENTURE and camping on unknown planets," he explained. "But it's also useful for any mouse who needs to POWER a laptop computer, or CHARGE an interstellar phone, or ILLUMINATE Christmas lights, or . . ."

BEEP! BEEEP! BEEEEP!

Black holey galaxies, it was my wrist phone again! It was Benjamin and Bugsy Wugsy, and they were waiting for me at the amousement park. I quickly said good-bye to the professor and jumped into another ASTROTAXI.

When I arrived, Benjamin and Bugsy Wugsy were so HAPPY to see me, they both gave me enormouse hugs!

"Thanks for coming," Benjamin squeaked happily.

Huh?
Puff, puff . . .

"YOU'RE THE BEST, UNCLE G!" added Bugsy Wugsy. What sweet little mouselets! I was almost moved to tears. But then I caught sight of something that really did bring tears to my eyes: the totally terrifying Transgalactic Tornado! It's the most FUR-RAISING attraction at Astral Park!

It's a roller coaster so TALL and so LONG and so terrifying that just thinking about it makes my whiskers quiver with fright. And as if that weren't enough,

WATERFALLS throughout the ride douse the riders at every turn! That's why every mouse who rides receives a free waterproof jacket.

Benjamin and Bugsy Wugsy couldn't wait to go on the roller coaster. And even though I was SCARED out of my fur, I agreed to ride it. What could I do? I can never say NO to friends and family, especially my nephew Benjamin!

I climbed aboard and squeezed my eyes SHUT. I didn't intend to open them until the ride was OVER. But right when we reached the highest curve . . .

BEEP! BEEEP!

BEEEEP!

Yay!
Ahhhhh!

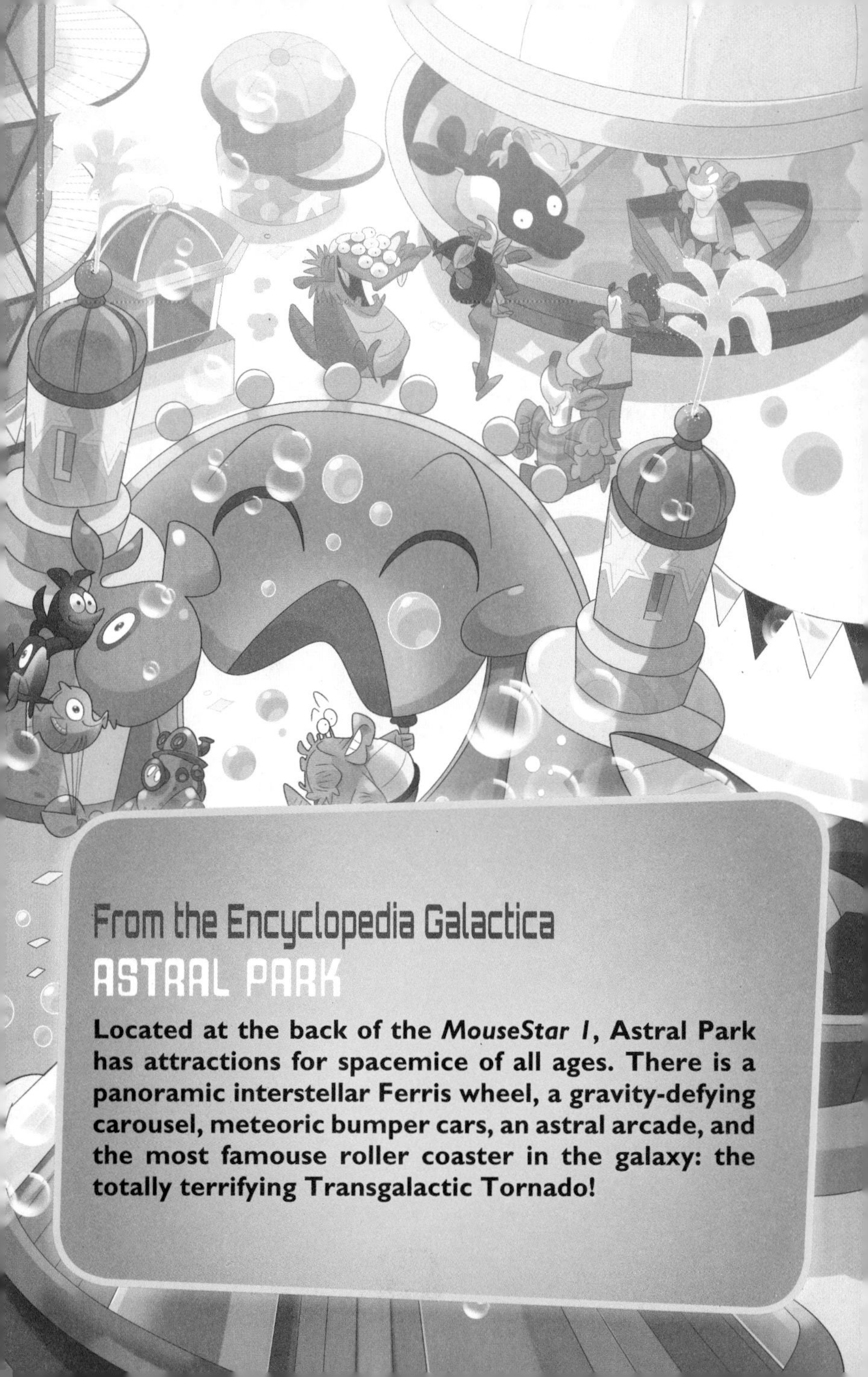

From the Encyclopedia Galactica

ASTRAL PARK

Located at the back of the *MouseStar 1*, Astral Park has attractions for spacemice of all ages. There is a panoramic interstellar Ferris wheel, a gravity-defying carousel, meteoric bumper cars, an astral arcade, and the most famouse roller coaster in the galaxy: the totally terrifying Transgalactic Tornado!

It was my wrist phone again! And this time, it was a real emergency!

"**Yellow alert!**" my sister, Thea, squeaked into the phone. "Geronimo, report to the control room immediately! Hurry!"

Then she hung up the phone without giving me any more information. And to think this was supposed to be my **day off**!

YELLOW ALERT!

What does a yellow alert mean? It means:

EMERGENCY! DANGER!
IMMINENT DISASTER!

In other words, it's one of those times that day off or no DAY OFF, the captain has to skedaddle to the control room right away. So for the third time that day, I stopped an astrotaxi and we hopped in. But this time, the driver tried to refuse us!

Why? It was simple. We were wearing waterproof jackets and we were totally drenched from the tips of our whiskers to the tips of our tails!

"You're ruining the seats of my taxi!" the driver complained.

I tried to explain the situation, but he wasn't paying attention.

"Listen, driver!" I finally blurted out. "I'm Captain Stiltonix. We're in a yellow alert! Take me immediately to the liftrix elevator to the control room!"

He stared at me in total surprise. "CAPTAIN STILTONIX? Is that really you? I didn't recognize you in that YELLOW JACKET and those soaking-wet clothes! Don't worry, though! I'll take care of you!"

He grabbed the controls of the astrotaxi and a nanosecond later, he had dropped us off at the nearest LIFTRIX. When the door of the control room opened, everyone turned to look at us.

My cousin Trap's eyes almost popped out of their sockets with shock. My sister,

Thea, just stared at me without saying a word. Grandfather William shook his head with DISAPPOINTMENT. And even Sally de Wrench, our ship's official mechanic and the loveliest rodent on the *MouseStar 1*, had a very SURPRISED expression on her snout! I felt so HUMILIATED.

Rescue Mission to Planet Polarix

In my rush to get to the control room, I hadn't thought to change out of my WET clothes. How I wished I was in my WARM, DRY uniform! Instead, I was dripping like a wet umbrella after a METEORIC rainstorm.

"Geronimo, what's going on?" my grandfather barked at me. "Where is your captain's UNIFORM?"

"Sorry, Grandfather," I mumbled. "There was the tennis lesson, then the tournament, and the laboratory, and then that frightening roller coaster!"

"That's no excuse!" he growled. "A captain must always be ready for every possibility — even a yellow alert!"

At that moment I remembered why I had rushed to the control room so QUICKLY.

"What happened?" I asked. "Is the MOUSESTAR 1 about to explode? Is a meteor heading toward us? Did we run out of GORGONZOLA cheese?"

"No, of course not!" Grandfather scoffed. "It's much worse than that. We're in the middle of an intergalactic video call with the president of the Interplanetary Scientific Research Institute, Professor Boris Astrowhiskers from the planet PHOTOSYNTHESON.

He has a very serious situation."

When I looked up at the plasma megascreen, I saw a TALL, THIN rodent wearing a white lab coat. Like Professor Greenfur, he was a vegetal mousoid, with fur covered in leaves.

PROFESSOR BORIS ASTROWHISKERS

"Greetings, professor Astrowhiskers!" I said. "My name is Stiltonix, Geronimo Stiltonix. I am the captain of the *MouseStar 1*."

The professor nodded, shaking his FOLIAGE.

"I'm truly happy to make your acquaintance, Captain Stiltonix," he replied politely. "I have heard so much about you from others across the galaxy!"

"What can I do for you?" I asked.

He **SIGHED**. "The reason I contacted you is that my friend and colleague Doctor Oslo Bonsai has *disappeared*! He was leading a SCIENTIFIC expedition with two of his assistants on the frozen planet of **Polarix**, and it's been days since I've heard from him. I don't know what to do! We Photosynthesons are studious, academic mice. We're not **ADVENTURE-SEEKING** spacemice like all of you on the **MOUSESTAR 1**!"

They've disappeared . . .

Huh?
Gasp!

"We would be happy to help," I REASSURED him.

Professor Astrowhiskers's LEAVES perked up with relief.

"I don't know how to thank you!" he exclaimed. "Captain Stiltonix, despite your, er, very STRANGE clothing, you are a REMARKABLE rodent!"

My snout turned red with embarrassment, but the professor didn't seem to notice. He went on to describe the details of the scientific expedition, including the location where Doctor Bonsai and his assistants had been gathering data when they DISAPPEARED.

When we ended our conversation, the megascreen went DARK.

"Spacemice, get ready for departure!" I ordered the crew. "We're going on a **rescue mission**!"

I set the engines to *WARP SPEED*. Then I turned to Trap.

"Cousin, keep an eye on the astral compass and set a steady course for the *planet Polarix*!" I told him.

"Aye, aye, Captain!" my cousin replied with a wink.

"Thea, I leave you in command of the MOUSESTAR 1," I told my sister. "I'm going to . . . ahem . . . change my clothes!"

I headed to my cabin. The notes for my book were right there on my desk. I sighed. My writing would just have to WAIT. We

were going on an important rescue mission to the planet Polarix! And to think this was supposed to have been my **day off**!

A True Captain!

When I got back to the control room, I was wearing my clean, **PRESSED** uniform. My **fur** had been combed, and *MouseStar 1* had arrived at its destination: the **PLANET POLARIX**!

My sister, Thea, was executing the maneuvers to dock within the planet's orbit, and I immediately noticed that the entire surface was covered with **snow** and **ice**.

BRRRRRR!

Polarix looked like an inhospitable and very **COLD** planet!

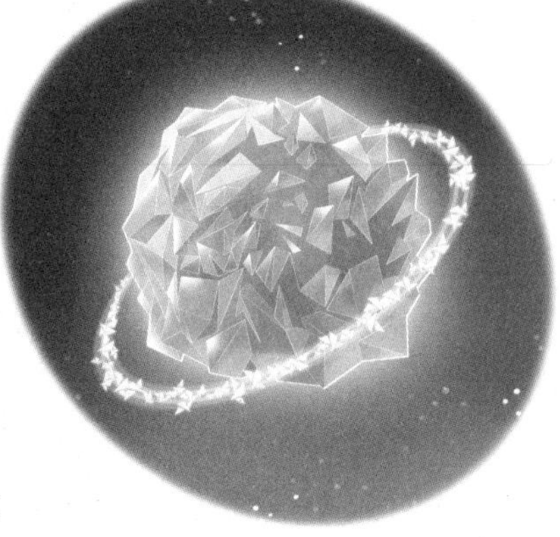

Just looking at that giant sphere of ice sent

CHILLS running down my tail. I was about to return to my cabin to change into my winter uniform (it's made completely of WOOL!) when the loudspeakers shrilled:

"Yellow alert!
Yellow alert!
Yellow alert!"

Martian mozzarella! What now? A new yellow alert? I looked at Thea, thinking maybe she had pushed the ALARM button, but she seemed as puzzled as I was.

"Did you pull the alarm?" I asked Trap.

But he shook his head, PERPLEXED.

Grandfather stamped his paw in frustration.

"Grandson!" he squeaked, pointing to the control panels. "Can't you see that the alarm is coming from the ENGINE ROOM? You need to contact SALLY at once!"

My snout turned as red as a Martian

space rock! BLACK HOLEY GALAXIES, why does my grandfather always make me look like a Neptuna fish? But Grandfather was right: The engine room's control panel light was FLASHING. I quickly contacted Sally.

"Captain, we have a problem!" she replied. "We can't proceed with the approach to Polarix. We need to TURN BACK!"

"What?" I replied. "What did you say? Turn back? No! We can't abandon Doctor Bonsai and his assistants. Professor Astrowhiskers is counting on us!"

"Captain, I'm afraid that I must INSIST!" Sally replied. "If we go any closer to Polarix, the *MouseStar 1*'s tetrastellium batteries will be destroyed! For some reason, it's as if an invisible force is sucking away our battery power. Either we turn around immediately or we won't have enough STELLAR ENERGY to leave here ever again!"

Galactic Gorgonzola! We were in real trouble. For the good of *MouseStar 1* and for the safety of the crew, we had to ZOOM away as fast as our SPACESHIP could carry us!

From the Encyclopedia Galactica

TETRASTELLIUM

This very precious, rare element is essential to space travel. The *MouseStar I* can whiz around the galaxies thanks to powerful tetrastellium batteries.

But I had given Professor Astrowhiskers my word that I would rescue Doctor Bonsai and his team! And I **ALWAYS** keep my promises.

"I have an idea!" I told Sally. "Get the **TELETRANSPORTIX** ready!"

Then I explained my plan to Thea.

"I will travel to Polarix with Trap and Professor Greenfur," I told her.

"What about the *MouseStar 1*?" she asked.

"Set a course for a nearby galaxy, but stay at a safe distance from **Polarix**," I explained. "We'll search for the **MISSING** scientists. Once we've located them, you can teletransport us back to the *MouseStar 1* — and to safety!"

Thea placed her paw on my shoulder in admiration.

"You're a true captain, Geronimo!" she squeaked approvingly.

My cousin Trap felt differently, though. He kept restlessly pacing BACK and FORTH across the control room.

"Come on, Trap," I said. "Let's head for the TELETRANSPORTIX. Hurry!"

No, no, no!

"No, no, no!" Trap replied, *shaking* his snout. "Dear cousin and captain, I have faith in you. But I wouldn't let myself be teletransported to that FROZEN planet even if I were competing in an interplanetary figure-skating competition!"

"There are three researchers whose lives are in danger," I pleaded with my cousin. "For the love of science, if we don't help them, they'll turn into MOUSICLES!"

But Trap wouldn't budge.

"Forget about it," he squeaked. "**I'm not coming!**"

I didn't know what to say. When Trap doesn't want to do something, he can be as stubborn as a **space mule** from the Pony Galaxy! But for once, Grandfather lent me a *paw*. He turned to look Trap straight in the eyes.

"As sure as my name is **William Stiltonix**, I command you, Trap Stilton, to explore that **UNKNOWN** planet!" he barked.

From the Encyclopedia Galactica

SPACE MULE FROM THE PONY GALAXY

The space mule from the Pony Galaxy is an animal that's very, very, very stubborn! When it decides not to move, it plants its feet down and no one can move it—not even an inch!

Trap immediately scampered toward the teletransportix room as *meekly* as a **SPACE SHEEP** from the planet Baa. Nobody dares to contradict **Grandfather**, not even my wise-mouse cousin Trap!

From the Encyclopedia Galactica

SPACE SHEEP FROM THE PLANET BAA

This animal has a thick bluish wool coat and a very cute face. It is particularly famouse for its mild and docile disposition. A space sheep will meekly follow any mouse who stops to greet it and give it a pat on the head.

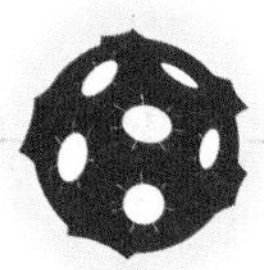

Lost in Hyperspace

We HURRIED to the teletransportix, leaped onto the platform, and waited for Sally to beam us to the FROZEN planet.

"How long do you want to stay on Polarix, Captain?" Sally asked me.

"No longer than we have to!" Trap muttered under his breath. "I'd say ten MICROASTROSECONDS!"

"I'm not sure how long our MISSION will take," I replied. "But I'll contact you on my wrist phone when we're ready. And if you don't hear from us within TWELVE HOURS, beam us back!"

We were ready for departure.

"Captain, just so you know, we need to compensate for the scarcity of tetrastellium

with a greater intracellular synchronized—"

I held up a paw to STOP her.

"Would you please simplify that?" I asked.

"Well, I'll try," Sally said with a SIGH. "Basically, you'll be fine in the end, but you may lose a few WHISKERS along the way!"

YIKES! Lose a few whiskers?! I was about to scream "*I want to get off!*" but Sally had already activated the commands. Then, suddenly, I heard Sally shout.

"NOOOOOOOOOOOOO!"

Out of the corner of my eye, I saw Benjamin and Bugsy Wugsy jump onto the teletransportix launchpad.

"We're coming too!" Benjamin cried out.

"Yeah!" Bugsy Wugsy exclaimed.

Nooooo! Stop!
Huh?
We're coming too!

Oh no! They had hitched a ride on our rescue mission!

"STOP!" I squeaked. "It's too DANGEROUS!"

But it was too late.

"There's too much WEIGHT on the launchpad now," Sally warned us. "You're at risk of getting lost in hyperspace!"

"Lost in hyperspace?" I cried. "Help! I want to get off! I GET REALLY, REALLY SPACESICK IN HYPERSPAAAAAACE!"

The Ice Planet Polarix

When I felt my paws land on something SOLID, I slowly opened my eyes. We had **rematerialized**. But where were we? Everything was **DARK**!

"Professor Greenfur? Trap? Benjamin? Bugsy?" I asked in **alarm**. "Where are we? Can someone turn on the **LIGHTS**?"

"Of course, Captain," answered Professor Greenfur. A moment later, the scientist lit the emergency **flashlight** powered by concentrated tetrastellium that he always carries with him. "I hope it lasts long enough for us to explore the **planet**."

A beam of light **LIT UP** a small room full of test tubes and plant samples.

"It's Doctor Bonsai's portable laboratory on the Polarix space base!" Professor Greenfur exclaimed.

By the **light** of the flashlight, I checked myself to make sure I had rematerialized properly. I took stock of every body part: Whiskers? Check! Paws? Check! Tail . . . tail? **Taaail?!**

Cosmic cheddar! I had lost my tail in hyperspace!

A moment later, I felt a sharp **pinch** on what felt like my tail. It was my cousin.

"I really don't understand why Grandfather William put you in command of

the MOUSESTAR 1 instead of me," Trap said with a SIGH. "Can't you see your tail is just tangled up in your uniform?"

I FELT LIKE SUCH A FOOL!

"Benjamin, would you please help me untangle my tail?" I asked SHEEPISHLY.

There was no reply. Frantically, I looked around for Benjamin and Bugsy Wugsy.

"Mouselings, where are you?" I squeaked.

Trap and Professor Greenfur tried calling out for them, too. NOTHING. There wasn't even a whisker's trace of my little nephew and his friend!

"Let's contact the *MouseStar 1*," I suggested. "Maybe they didn't make it onto the launchpad after all!"

But Professor Greenfur shook his head sadly with a loud, leafy rustle.

"Captain, there's no SIGNAL!" he told me. "We can't communicate with *MouseStar 1* or with the mouselings. Our only hope is that they rematerialized somewhere else and didn't get lost in hyperspace!"

A chill ran down my **tail**.

MARTIAN MOZZARELLA!

This rescue mission was turning out to be a **disaster**. It was a real possibility that Benjamin and Bugsy Wugsy were *lost in hyperspace*!

This Way . . . No, That Way!

Benjamin and Bugsy had to be somewhere on the Polarix space base. I COULD FEEL IT IN MY FUR!

But tracking them down wouldn't be easy. We still hadn't been able to SWITCH ON the lights. And as if that weren't enough, my cousin Trap kept NEEDLING me.

"I told you it would have been better for us to stay in our own WARM ship," he grumbled. "We could be cozily gnawing some delectable CHEESES right now, but instead, we're freezing our tails off in

the dark here on Polarix!"

Maybe Trap wasn't altogether wrong. We searched the space base by the light of Professor Greenfur's emergency flashlight but couldn't find any sign of Benjamin and Bugsy Wugsy. We didn't see a trace of Doctor Bonsai or his assistants, either. The base seemed to be completely DESERTED!

Suddenly, I thought I saw a movement behind us. I turned quickly, but there was NO ONE there. Still, it felt like someone was watching us!

"Did you see that?" I asked the others.

Trap shook his head. "I didn't see a thing."

"Well, what should we do now, Captain?" Professor Greenfur asked.

I froze. Oh, how I hate to be put on the spot! Everyone expects me to know what

to do since I'm the captain, but sometimes I just don't know!

"Well, let's go THIS WAY," I mumbled uncertainly. "No, let's go that way. Wait, let's actually go THIS WAY."

"Ouch!" Trap cried. "You stepped on my tail!"

"Sorry," I muttered. Even though we had the emergency flashlight, it was DARK enough

that we kept bumping into one another.

We tried the light switches again but had NO LUCK! So we stuck with the flashlight. Unfortunately, though, the BATTERIES were running very low.

"If only I had my new portable energy generator with me," Professor Greenfur said with a SIGH.

"Benjamin! Bugsy Wugsy! Doctor Bonsai!" we called. "IF YOU'RE HERE, PLEASE ANSWER!"

THIS WAY . . .

There were no

replies. Still, wherever we went, I had the feeling someone was WATCHING us.

I told Trap about my hunch.

"You're such a scaredy-mouse, Cousin!" he teased. "Just because we're on a STRANGE planet in an ABANDONED space base looking for missing rodents, you think we're being followed!"

With nothing else to do, I led my rescue mission team THIS WAY and that way all over the base. As we went along, we explored the following rooms:

1. THE GARBAGE ROOM, where I slipped on a banana peel and landed paws up on my tail. WHO would have left it there?

2. The bathroom, where our uniforms got soaked up to the knees because the floor was flooded. WHO would have left the faucets running?

3. THE SUPPLY ROOM full of tools and spare parts, where a hammer fell from above and landed on my paw. Ouch! WHO would have left it suspended over the door like that?

4. the boiler room, which was ice-cold instead of hot. WHO would have set the temperature to negative forty degrees?

Finally, we checked the dorms, the game room, and the radio station. Then we stumbled across a closet full of superaccessorized thermal suits used to explore the icy planet.

Three suits looked ready to put on. We could use them to explore the exterior of

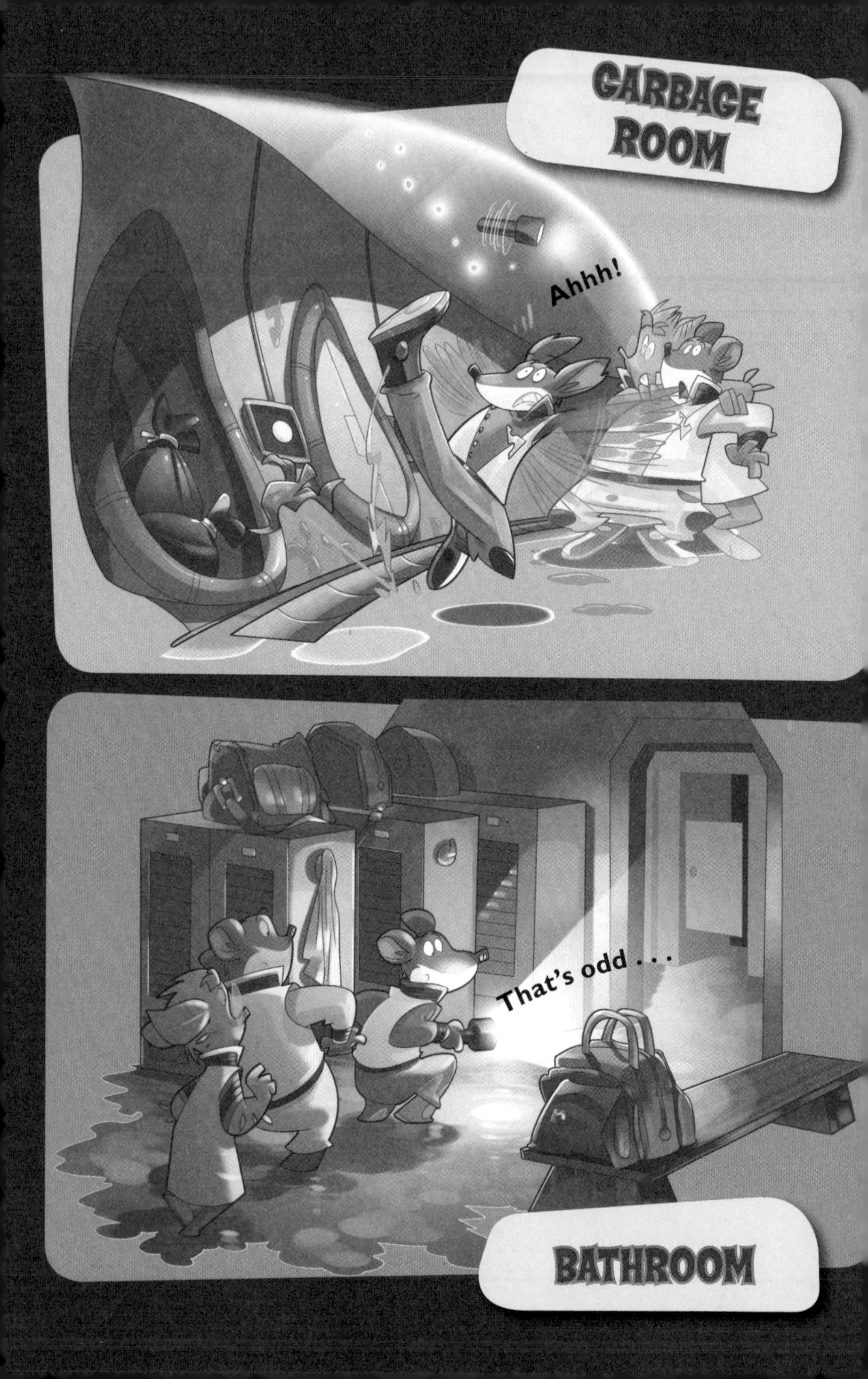
GARBAGE ROOM
Ahhh!
That's odd . . .
BATHROOM

SUPPLY ROOM
Gasp!
BOILER ROOM
Brrrr!

the space base without **FREEZING** while we searched for Benjamin, Bugsy Wugsy, and Doctor Bonsai and his assistants!

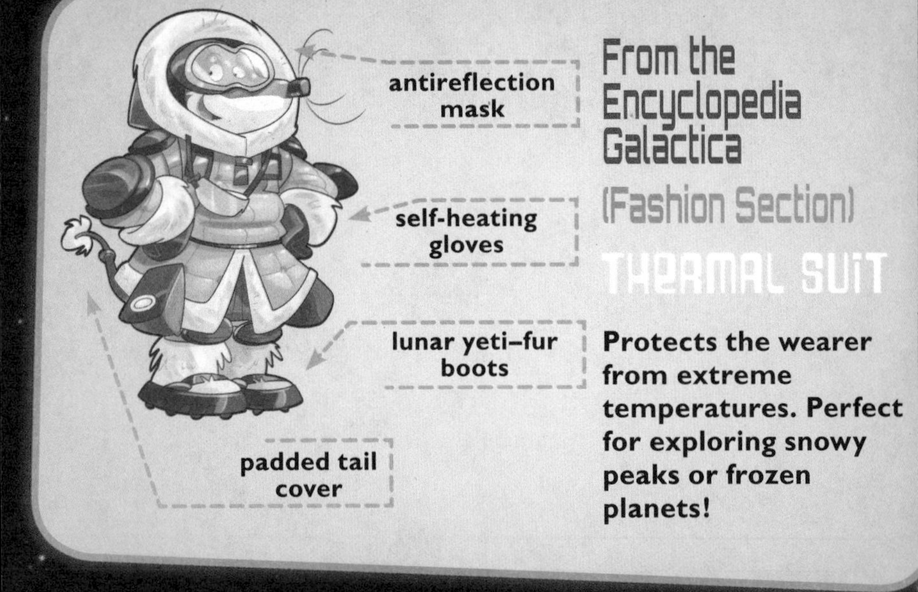

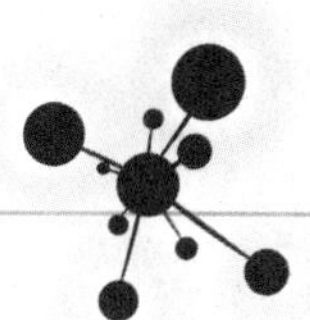

The Rainbow Cave

As we slipped the suits on, I had a sudden thought.

"What if Benjamin and Bugsy Wugsy REMATERIALIZED outside the base instead of inside?" I asked the professor. "They're not wearing suits like these."

"That's true," Professor Greenfur answered. "If that happened, they are certainly at risk of becoming mousicles!"

"Let's hurry then," I shouted. "If they're here, we have to find them QUICKLY!"

With that, we stepped out of the base and onto the FROZEN planet.

Cosmic Cheddar! It was snowing heavily outside, the wind was blowing, and

it was VERY cold! But we couldn't give up: We had to find Benjamin and Bugsy Wugsy, even if I had to sacrifice my own FUR! And hopefully we'd find the missing scientists on our search as well.

The SNOW and ice extended as far as the eye could see. We had made it a short distance from the base when I noticed a little cave in the ice. I pointed it out to Trap and Professor Greenfur, and we headed in that direction, fighting icy cold gusts of wind the entire way.

From the outside, the cave's entrance looked like no more than a tiny hole in the rock. But once we stepped inside, we were shocked to find that it was actually a spacious cavern full of pools of steaming hot water, making the cave surprisingly WARM!

It seemed as if we were in a gigantic spa!

A cave?
Follow me!

Huge stalactites hung from the ceiling, and stalagmites rose from the floor all around us. The stalagmites were surrounded by small mounds of brightly colored balls. We passed RED, YELLOW, ORANGE, blue, and more. Trap immediately reached out his PAW to grab a handful.

"Be careful!" Professor Greenfur warned. "We don't know what those are. They could be dangerous."

"These things?" Trap scoffed at us. "Dangerous? They're just LITTLE COLORED BALLS!"

Before the professor could reply, Trap had chosen a few to take with him.

Meanwhile, I kept thinking of Benjamin and Bugsy Wugsy. Where were they? I was very worried! I couldn't accept that they might have dematerialized or turned

Look!
Wow! It's warm in here!

into frozen little mousicles. But they were nowhere to be found.

"Let's head back to the base," I said with a SAD sigh. "The little mouselets aren't here, and neither are the scientists."

The Pluffs

We returned to the base and removed those uncomfortable **padded** suits. Trap could tell I was feeling unhappy.

"Don't worry, we'll find them," he reassured me. "In the meantime, let's get to the **kitchen** and cook up something **WARM**! I'm so hungry!"

The only question was: Which way was the kitchen? We hadn't seen it earlier. But Trap was up for the task. He just stuck his snout in the air.

Sniff!

SNIFF!

Sniff!

Believe it or not, my cousin used his nose to take us to the kitchen! And when we got there, we heard the strangest thing: There were muffled CRIES coming from one of the cupboards!

"HELP! HELP!" we heard faintly.

"WE'RE IN HERE! OPEN UP!"

I would have recognized those voices anywhere: It was my little nephew Benjamin and Bugsy Wugsy! We had finally found them! They leaped out of the cupboard when we opened it, and I hugged them both tightly.

"What are you doing in the pantry?" I asked. "Actually, first tell me what you're doing on this PLANET! I don't remember giving you PERMISSION to be part of this expedition!"

Now that the mouselings were SAFE, my disappointment in my nephew and his friend returned. They weren't even supposed to be here!

Benjamin lowered his EYES. "You're right, Uncle Geronimo," he admitted. "But it never SNOWS on *MouseStar 1*! Bugsy and I just wanted to have a little snowball fight."

I sighed. It was hard for me to stay angry with my SWEET little nephew for long.

"But we didn't **REMATERIALIZE** in the cupboard," added Bugsy Wugsy. "Someone shoved us inside it and **locked** the door with a key!"

"Someone did what?" I asked in shock. "But who? And why?"

I looked around **SUSPICIOUSLY**. So did Trap and Professor Greenfur. My cousin even tried a few **COSMO-KARATE** moves to scare off any would-be attackers! But there seemed to be no one there but US. I examined the cupboard, hoping to find a clue. Then I noticed a tuft of long, SILKY, colored fur that was caught on the doorknob. I was about to show it to Professor Greenfur when my cousin Trap burst into loud laughter.

A second later, the professor began GIGGLING. Then Benjamin and Bugsy Wugsy joined in. What did everyone find so funny? This was a very serious situation!

Then I saw it. There were seven colored puffs of fur jumping out of another cupboard: red, orange, yellow, green, BLUE, indigo, and violet, just like the colors of the RAINBOW! Their soft fur shone brightly. Then the strange little creatures began to sing:

"PLUFF, PLUFF, HEE, HEE, HEE! PLUFF, PLUFF, HO, HO, HO! PLUFF, PLUFF, HA, HA, HA!"

Pluff!

The strange little puffs continued to sing as they SKIPPED here and there. The orange one landed on Professor Greenfur's head and began SWINGING from one of his ears to the other!

"Aw, they're so cute!" Benjamin cooed.

"And they're so much fun!" Bugsy Wugsy agreed.

Even Trap was mesmerized by the TINY creatures.

He's so cute!
They're adorable!
Ha, ha, ha!

"Professor Greenfur, what are these aliens called?" I asked.

"Ha, ha, ha!" The professor laughed. "This little one is tickling me!" Then he became serious for a second.

"To answer your question, Captain, I'd call these aliens PLUFFS," the professor continued. "Seems like a good name, given their little song, don't you agree?"

"Look at this cute yellow guy," Bugsy Wugsy said, cuddling one of the pluffs. "He's so snuggly!"

I didn't understand the reason for all of the fuss, but since everyone insisted, I extended a friendly paw toward the yellow PLUFF. He came closer, but I didn't like the way he looked at me at all. For a second I thought he was going to BITE my paw! But before I could pull back, the alien jumped onto my arm and ran up to my ear. Then he started TICKLING me unmercifully!

"Give him your cheek, Uncle," Benjamin suggested. "It looks like he wants to give you a KISS!"

A kiss? Really? It looked to me like he wanted to CHOMP my snout! But I didn't want to be rude to the little creature, so I leaned CLOSER. The pluff leaned toward me. Suddenly, I began SNEEZING uncontrollably.

"ACHOO! ACHOO! ACHOO!"

ACHOO!

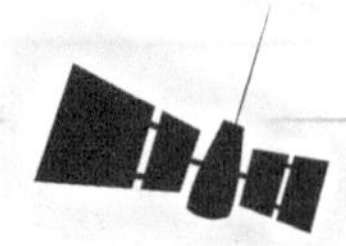

Come On, Let's Take Them with Us!

I couldn't seem to stop SNEEZING! It was as if I had a TERRIBLE cold.

"Professor Greenfur—ACHOO!" I asked between sneezes, "do you have—achoo!—anything for a COLD? Achoo!"

"Sorry, Captain," the Professor replied, a dreamy look in his eyes. "I don't have time to look. I'm busy combing this pluff's fur."

So I asked

Trap, Benjamin, and Bugsy Wugsy.

But Trap was busy playing with a little orange pluff, Benjamin was giving a few PLUFFS a bath in the kitchen sink, and Bugsy Wugsy was drying them off carefully. No one seemed the least bit concerned about me!

"But — achoo! — isn't anyone — achoo! — worried about my sudden COLD?" I asked my friends between very LOUD sneezes.

"Captain, I think I know what's wrong," the professor replied as he continued to play with the little pluffs. "You seem to be having an allergic reaction to the pluff fur!"

Trap came running over to me.

"If you're allergic, can I take your yellow PLUFF?" he asked.

"Achoo! Do whatever you want," I replied. "But please, take him away! Achoo!"

My cousin didn't have to be told TWICE. Trap took the ALIEN and snuggled it, covering it with kisses.

"Geronimo isn't a very FRIENDLY mouse," I heard Trap whisper to the little creature. "But I love you!"

The pluff rubbed itself affectionately against Trap's snout. Then it turned and SECRETLY stuck out its tongue at me!

IT DEFINITELY HAD SOMETHING AGAINST ME!

You're so cuddly!

There was something about the little pluffs that I didn't trust. I tried to WARN my team, but they all acted as though they were under some sort of pluff spell.

"They're so cute!" Professor Greenfur kept repeating.

"And so beautiful," Trap chimed in, a glazed look in his eyes.

"Uncle, can we take them back to the spaceship with us?" Benjamin asked.

"They could sleep in my dollhouse," Bugsy Wugsy offered. "I haven't played with it in a long time."

I was about to tell them no when I heard a creaking sound, as though someone was about to open a squeaky door. Then I heard the thud of approaching footsteps.

"We're in danger!" I alerted my friends. "There's someone in the hall!"

But no one seemed to notice. They all seemed hypnotized by the furry little aliens. The pluffs had started purring like cats as Trap, Professor Greenfur, Benjamin, and

Bugsy caressed them. And the more the creatures purred, the more everyone seemed to fall under the pluffs' SPELL.

"Let go of those pluffs!" I shouted DESPERATELY. "Quickly, let's run and hide!"

"But the pluffs are our friends," Professor Greenfur answered ROBOTICALLY.

"Whoever is not a friend of the pluffs is our enemy," Trap said, a DAZED expression on his snout.

Once again the yellow pluff turned toward me and stuck out his tongue before he went back to purring loudly along with the others.

A second later, the door OPENED . . .

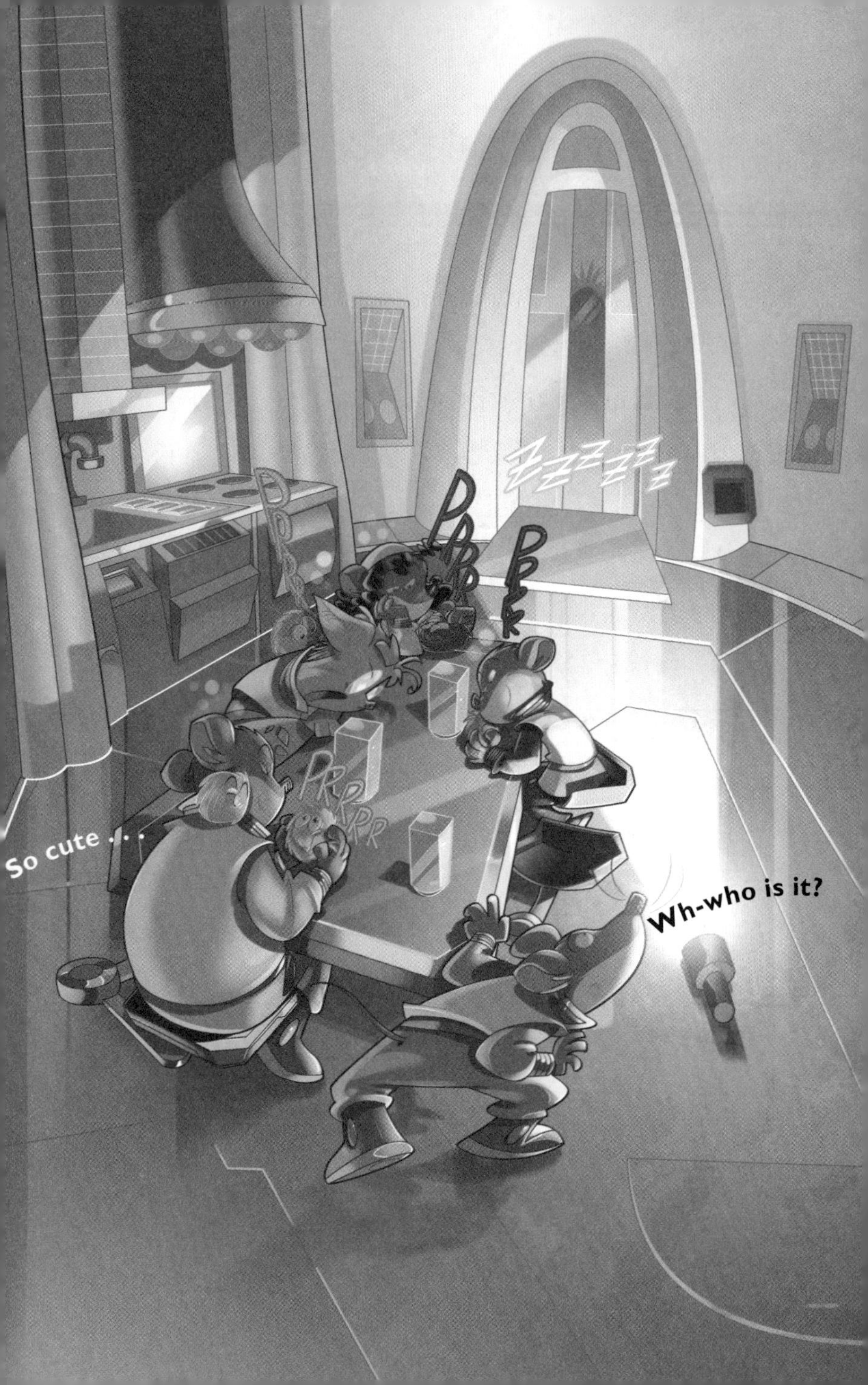
So cute . . .
Wh-who is it?

HOLEY CRATERS!

The sound of those footsteps in the hall made my fur **freeze**. Who could it be? Was it a **space mummy** from Uranus? Or maybe a Martian **ZOMBIE**?

Either way, I thought for sure that our fur was fried. We were **goners**!

But a second later, I found myself snout-to-snout with . . . **DOCTOR OSLO BONSAI** and his two assistants!

"Doctor Bonsai!" I exclaimed in relief, putting out my paw. "I'm **Captain Stiltonix**. Professor Boris Astrowhiskers sent my crew to **search** for you! Are you all right?"

I expected a **PAWSHAKE** or maybe even a grateful hug, but instead, I got nothing! Doctor Bonsai's eyes looked as glazed over as everyone else's. He picked up our flashlight from the ground.

"Why isn't the rodent with the GREEN suit hypnotized like the others?" he asked the orange pluff that was perched on his shoulder.

HOLEY CRATERS! He was talking about me!

The yellow pluff next to Trap answered him:

"HEE, HEE, HEE! HA, HA, HA! HO, HO, HO! ACHOO! ACHOO! ACHOO!"

Doctor Bonsai seemed to understand, even though I had no idea what the little creature had said.

"We must capture him!" Doctor Bonsai said to his assistants. "Now!"

Then the scientist grabbed me by the **paws**.

"Wait!" I protested. "Doctor Bonsai, I'm the captain of **MOUSESTAR 1**! I'm your friend. I came here to take you home."

Suddenly, I realized that the orange pluff by

Bonsai's ear was giving him orders! And the strange little fuzzy aliens had hypnotized his assistants, too!

I tried to escape, but it was USELESS! Doctor Bonsai and his assistants held me very, very, very TIGHTLY. They headed for the door that led outside, DRAGGING me with them. The members of my team followed us like robots. They seemed to be following the aliens' orders now, too!

I was sure they were going to leave us out in the cold until we turned into frozen mousicles. Instead, they took us back to the CAVE where Trap had collected the little colored balls. An enormouse surprise awaited us there!

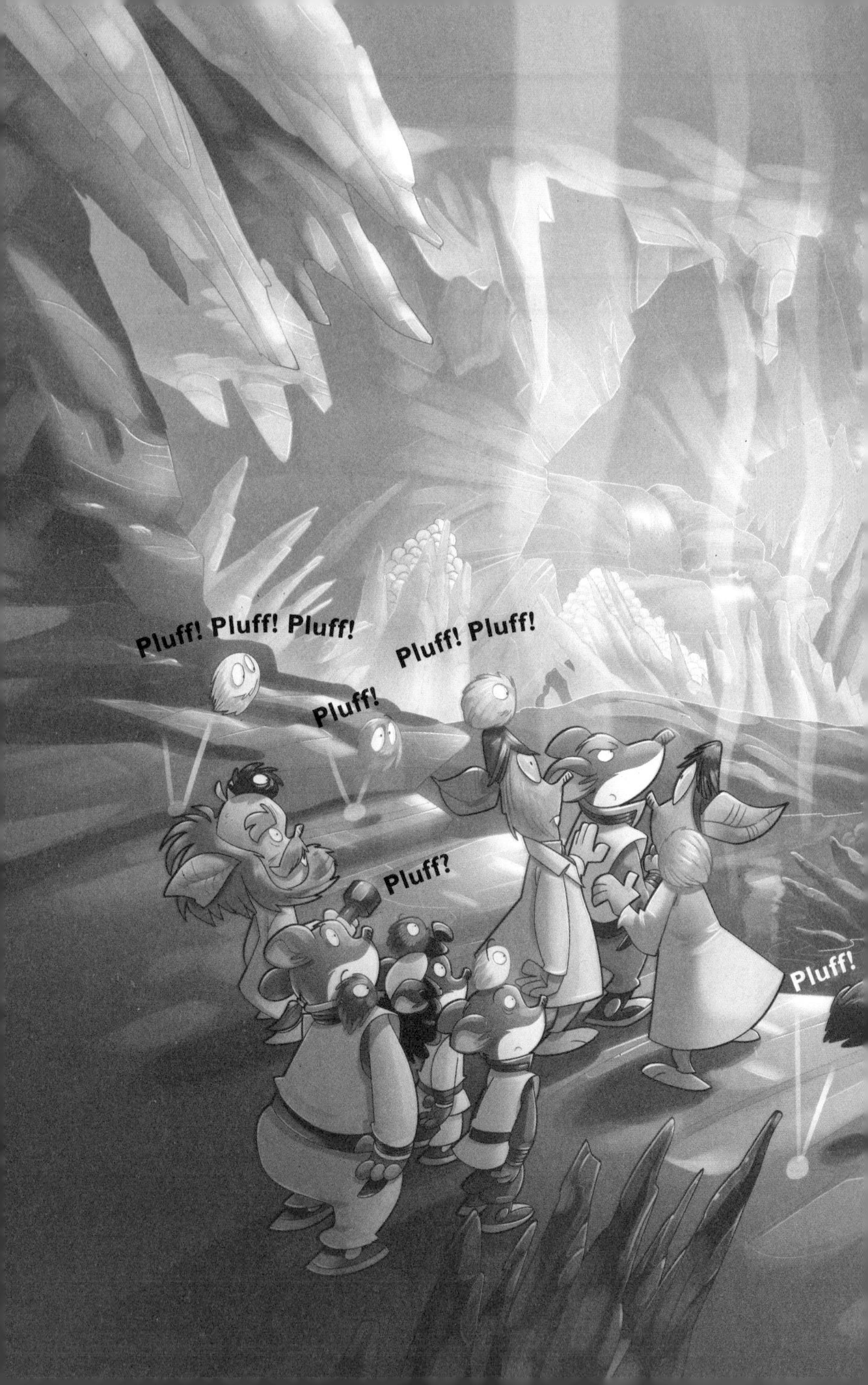
Pluff! Pluff! Pluff!
Pluff! Pluff!
Pluff!
Pluff?
Pluff!

Good for you, my little pluffs!
Pluff!
Pluff! Pluff!

THE QUEEN OF THE PLUFFS

A GIANT pluff was waiting for us in the middle of the cave. Like the others, it was extremely furry. But instead of being one solid color, it had stripes of all the colors of the RAINBOW.

Cosmic cheddar chunks!

The large pluff looked very intimidating! It sat on what looked like a rock THRONE.

As soon as I got close to the giant pluff, my nostrils began to ITCH uncontrollably and I started to sneeze.

"Achoo! Achoo! Achoo!"

The little yellow pluff whispered something to the giant MULTICOLORED pluff, who turned to me with a very angry

expression on its face. It looked as if it absolutely had something against me! I opened my mouth to squeak, but the only thing that came out was:

"ACHOO!"

The giant pluff barked:

"HEE, HEE, HEE, HEE, HEE!
HO, HA, HA! PLUFF!
HA, HEE, HEE, HO!"

Doctor Bonsai turned to me with vacant eyes and translated in a mechanical voice:

"The queen of the pluffs is furious! She says that we scientists have built a scientific base on Polarix without asking her permission. And furthermore, she says the rodent in the yellow uniform has stolen seven of her precious EGGS: one of each COLOR!"

Galactic Gorgonzola! She was talking

about my cousin Trap and the **BALLS** he had picked up in the cave! Only they weren't balls . . . they were **UNHATCHED** pluff eggs! I realized that's why I had felt as if someone had been watching me all around the Polarix base. The **ALIENS** had been keeping an eye on us since our arrival!

"The queen of the pluffs says the only good thing we brought to her planet is tetrastellium, which she likes very much," Doctor Bonsai continued.

But why would the pluffs need tetrastellium? I would have happily given them some if I had any, but I

didn't have the TINIEST speck!

"If you let us return to our spaceship—ACHOO!—we will gladly let you have all the tetrastellium at the science base—ACHOO!" I offered.

"HEE, HEE, HEE, HOOO!" replied the queen.

"HEE, HEE, HEE, HOOO!" repeated the little yellow pluff.

"She said not to bother trying to trick her!" Doctor Bonsai translated. "She knows very well that the base's tetrastellium is gone, because she's the one who used it all up!"

Black holey galaxies! So that's why the lights at the BASE hadn't worked. The pluffs had used up all the tetrastellium—and trashed the place after it was gone. And that explained why the entire planet of POLARIX

had given off an INVISIBLE force that sucked away the *MouseStar 1*'s battery power. The pluffs were so greedy for tetrastellium that they would have DESTROYED our spaceship if Sally hadn't turned back in time.

Doctor Bonsai turned on Professor Greenfur's flashlight and pointed it at the cave floor. The little aliens began to dance happily in the beam of light.

The queen of the pluffs spoke again, this time in our language.

"RODENTS, YOU ARE MY PRISONERS!" she said. "Bring your spaceship here immediately! If your friends want you back, tell them to pay a ransom of one and a half trillion astropounds of tetrastellium. If this ransom is not met, you will all be turned into MOUSICLES!"

I shuddered. One and a half trillion astropounds is an ENORMOUSE quantity! Even if I scraped the very bottom of all of *MouseStar 1*'s reservoirs, we'd never be able to satisfy the ransom request.

WE WERE GONERS! Good-bye to warm, CHEDDAR-SCENTED bubble baths. Our fur was about to be FROZEN for all eternity!

I looked at Professor Greenfur, Trap, and the mouselings, hoping one of them would come up with an escape plan. But they were all still hypnotized by the pluffs' loud purring sounds. I guessed the queen had put us under her SPELL to keep us from trying to escape. But that didn't explain why I was unaffected by the little ALIENS.

I tried to stall.

"Um, can I ask why—ACHOO!—you need all this—ACHOO!—tetrastellium? ACHOO!"

"It's very simple," the queen of the pluffs explained. "Our planet is FROZEN solid. In

HA, HA, HA!

HEH, HEH, HEH!

order to **SURVIVE**, we have to live in dark caves like this one. But with tetrastellium, we can light our caves. **WE LIKE LIGHT! IT MAKES US HAPPY!** So we need more tetrastellium!"

I looked at the pluffs gathered around the flashlight and realized it was TRUE. They had begun to sing a weird but pleasant tune, and **SWAYED** with the rhythm of the music. They seemed so HAPPY!

Beep! Beeep! Beeeep!

I wasn't sure what to do. How did I always manage to get myself into these MESSES? I was contemplating my next move when suddenly . . .

BEEP! BEEEP!
BEEEEP!

The timer on my wrist phone began beeping! How fast time flew — there were only a few minutes left before the **twelve hours** were up. Sally was about to use the teletransportix to rescue us. Perfect timing!

I took advantage of the fact that the pluffs were distracted by the flashlight, and I

crept toward Benjamin. His eyes were glazed over and he stared at the aliens, completely hypnotized. Bugsy Wugsy, Trap, and the scientists were hypnotized as well. I had to figure out a way to WAKE them. It was too DANGEROUS to teletransport them in that condition!

So I stretched out my paw and gave Benjamin's tail a sharp pinch. Nothing! I tried pinching him harder. Still nothing! I tried again, but it still didn't work. NOTHING HAPPENED!

Then I had an idea. I reached up and pulled out one of my own whiskers — ouch! Why? Simple! I used it to tickle my nephew's snout! A second later, Benjamin sneezed.

"Achoo! Achoo! Achoo!"

He snapped out of the trance! I took my whisker and went around to Trap, Bugsy Wugsy,

Professor Greenfur, Doctor Bonsai, and his assistants. And it worked—SNEEZING made them all wake up.

"Let's make a run for it!" I shouted to them. "Hurry! Before it's too late!"

But the **PLUFFS** had realized we were free. They began to close in on us menacingly. I looked at the timer on my watch:

Ten . . . nine . . . eight . . .

The queen of the pluffs rolled toward us in an angry ball of **rainbow-colored** fluff.

"Stop!" she shouted. "You belong to me now, mice!"

I grabbed Bugsy Wugsy and Trap. "Quickly!" I squeaked. "Let's all **HOLD** paws!"

The countdown had almost ended.

Three . . . two . . . one . . .

The queen of the pluffs was about to roll right into us when suddenly everything went **DARK**.

As promised, Sally had teletransported us back onto the **MOUSESTAR 1**. We were safe!

"Mission accomplished!" we all shouted. **"SPACEMICE FOR ONE, SPACEMICE FOR ALL!"**

VRROOOOOOMMMM!
BZZZZZZZZZZ!
Aaaaahhhhhhh!

Greetings from the Rainbow Planet

When we rematerialized in the control room, the *MouseStar 1* crew welcomed us like heroes. Even Grandfather William gave me his CONGRATULATIONS! I felt like a real captain. Trap helped me take off my gear.

"Don't let it get into your head, Cousin," he commented. "You were just LUCKY. If it weren't for your allergy to the pluffs, they would have turned us all into **mousicles**!"

At the word **ALLERGY**, I began sneezing all over again!

"ACHOO! ACHOO! ACHOO!"

HOLEY CRATERS! My sneezes

Congratulations!
CLAP
CLAP CLAP CLAP
Our heroes!
Well done!

CLAP
CLAP
ACHOO!
CLAP
CLAP
Way to go!

could only mean one thing—there was a pluff onboard the spaceship. We were in great danger! I had to sound the yellow alert!

"ACHOO! ACHOO!" I shouted. "Code—achoo!—yellow! Furry little alien onboard! ACHOO! ACHOO!"

I glanced at Benjamin and Bugsy Wugsy, thinking they had hidden a little pluff in one of their pockets. But Benjamin immediately denied it.

"We have nothing to do with it!" he said. "Even if we had really, really wanted one, we learned our lesson."

"It's true," Bugsy Wugsy agreed. "The pluffs are cute and FUNNY, but they're not toys! They're little alien creatures, and they should be left alone to live in peace on their own planet."

Well said! What BRIGHT little rodents. I wanted to tell Benjamin and Bugsy Wugsy how much I appreciated them, but the only thing I could say was:

"ACHOO! ACHOO! ACHOO!"

Trap elbowed me. "Stop all that sneezing, Cousin, or you'll have a DIPLOMATIC incident to deal with," he teased. "Don't you see you're also ALLERGIC to Doctor Bonsai and his assistants' foliage?"

Martian mozzarella! So that was the reason for my uncontrollable sneezing! I looked around for Professor Greenfur in the hope that he knew of a cure. But he was gone! I searched for him all over the spaceship. Finally, I bumped into him in the hallway, where he stood gazing DREAMILY out into space through the ship's porthole.

"Look at that beautiful RAINBOW, Captain," he said with a sigh.

I peeked through the window and saw a spectacular rainbow stretching over POLARIX'S atmosphere.

"But how is that possible?" I whispered. "Where did it come from?"

"I used the teletransportix to send the PLUFFS my latest invention: the portable stellar energy generator! With it, they can light their caves. Now they can go on singing and dancing happily!"

"Good for you, Professor!" I commended him. "But why the rainbow?"

"The generator's light filters through the planet's ice and breaks up into

the seven colors of the rainbow," he explained. "Isn't nature AMAZING, Captain?"

We remained there in silence as we watched Polarix and the rainbow slowly move farther and farther away from our spaceship until the icy planet was just a tiny dot.

When I got back to my cabin, the NOVEL I was writing was waiting for me on my desk, right where I had left it. I sighed.

Maybe tomorrow will be a better day for writing, I thought. Then I hung this note on the door before I climbed into bed:

Don't miss any adventures of the Spacemice!

#1 Alien Escape

#2 You're Mine, Captain!

#3 Ice Planet Adventure

Up Next!

#4 The Galactic Goal

Be sure to read all my fabumouse adventures!
#1 Lost Treasure of the Emerald Eye
#2 The Curse of the Cheese Pyramid
#3 Cat and Mouse in a Haunted House
#4 I'm Too Fond of My Fur!
#5 Four Mice Deep in the Jungle
#6 Paws Off, Cheddarface!
#7 Red Pizzas for a Blue Count
#8 Attack of the Bandit Cats
#9 A Fabumouse Vacation for Geronimo
#10 All Because of a Cup of Coffee
#11 It's Halloween, You 'Fraidy Mouse!
#12 Merry Christmas, Geronimo!
#13 The Phantom of the Subway
#14 The Temple of the Ruby of Fire
#15 The Mona Mousa Code
#16 A Cheese-Colored Camper
#17 Watch Your Whiskers, Stilton!
#18 Shipwreck on the Pirate Islands
#19 My Name Is Stilton, Geronimo Stilton
#20 Surf's Up, Geronimo!

#21 The Wild, Wild West

#22 The Secret of Cacklefur Castle

A Christmas Tale

#23 Valentine's Day Disaster

#24 Field Trip to Niagara Falls

#25 The Search for Sunken Treasure

#26 The Mummy with No Name

#27 The Christmas Toy Factory

#28 Wedding Crasher

#29 Down and Out Down Under

#30 The Mouse Island Marathon

#31 The Mysterious Cheese Thief

Christmas Catastrophe

#32 Valley of the Giant Skeletons

#33 Geronimo and the Gold Medal Mystery

#34 Geronimo Stilton, Secret Agent

#35 A Very Merry Christmas

#36 Geronimo's Valentine

#37 The Race Across America

#38 A Fabumouse School Adventure

#39 Singing Sensation

#40 The Karate Mouse

#41 Mighty Mount Kilimanjaro

#42 The Peculiar Pumpkin Thief

#43 I'm Not a Supermouse!

Geronimo Stilton
THE GIANT DIAMOND ROBBERY
#44 The Giant Diamond Robbery
SAVE THE WHITE WHALE!
#45 Save the White Whale!
THE HAUNTED CASTLE
#46 The Haunted Castle
RUN FOR THE HILLS, GERONIMO!
#47 Run for the Hills, Geronimo!
THE MYSTERY IN VENICE
#48 The Mystery in Venice
THE WAY OF THE SAMURAI
#49 The Way of the Samurai
THIS HOTEL IS HAUNTED!
#50 This Hotel Is Haunted!
THE ENORMOUSE PEARL HEIST
#51 The Enormouse Pearl Heist
MOUSE IN SPACE!
#52 Mouse in Space!
RUMBLE IN THE JUNGLE
#53 Rumble in the Jungle
GET INTO GEAR, STILTON!
#54 Get into Gear, Stilton!
THE GOLDEN STATUE PLOT
#55 The Golden Statue Plot
FLIGHT OF THE RED BANDIT
#56 Flight of the Red Bandit
Special Edition!
THE HUNT FOR THE GOLDEN BOOK
The Hunt for the Golden Book
THE STINKY CHEESE VACATION
#57 The Stinky Cheese Vacation
THE SUPER CHEF CONTEST
#58 The Super Chef Contest
WELCOME TO MOLDY MANOR
#59 Welcome to Moldy Manor
Special Edition!
The Hunt for the Curious Cheese
THE TREASURE OF EASTER ISLAND
#60 The Treasure of Easter Island
Don't miss my journeys through time!
THE JOURNEY THROUGH TIME
BACK IN TIME
THE SECOND JOURNEY THROUGH TIME
SCHOLASTIC

Meet GERONIMO STILTONOOT

He is a cavemouse—Geronimo Stilton's ancient ancestor! He runs the stone newspaper in the prehistoric village of Old Mouse City. From dealing with dinosaurs to dodging meteorites, his life in the Stone Age is full of adventure!

#1 The Stone of Fire

#2 Watch Your Tail!

#3 Help, I'm in Hot Lava!

#4 The Fast and the Frozen

#5 The Great Mouse Race

#6 Don't Wake the Dinosaur!

#7 I'm a Scaredy-Mouse!

#8 Surfing for Secrets

Be sure to read all of our magical special edition adventures!

THE KINGDOM OF FANTASY

THE QUEST FOR PARADISE:
THE RETURN TO THE KINGDOM OF FANTASY

THE AMAZING VOYAGE:
THE THIRD ADVENTURE IN THE KINGDOM OF FANTASY

THE DRAGON PROPHECY:
THE FOURTH ADVENTURE IN THE KINGDOM OF FANTASY

THE VOLCANO OF FIRE:
THE FIFTH ADVENTURE IN THE KINGDOM OF FANTASY

THE SEARCH FOR TREASURE:
THE SIXTH ADVENTURE IN THE KINGDOM OF FANTASY

THE ENCHANTED CHARMS:
THE SEVENTH ADVENTURE IN THE KINGDOM OF FANTASY

THEA STILTON: THE JOURNEY TO ATLANTIS

THEA STILTON: THE SECRET OF THE FAIRIES

THEA STILTON: THE SECRET OF THE SNOW

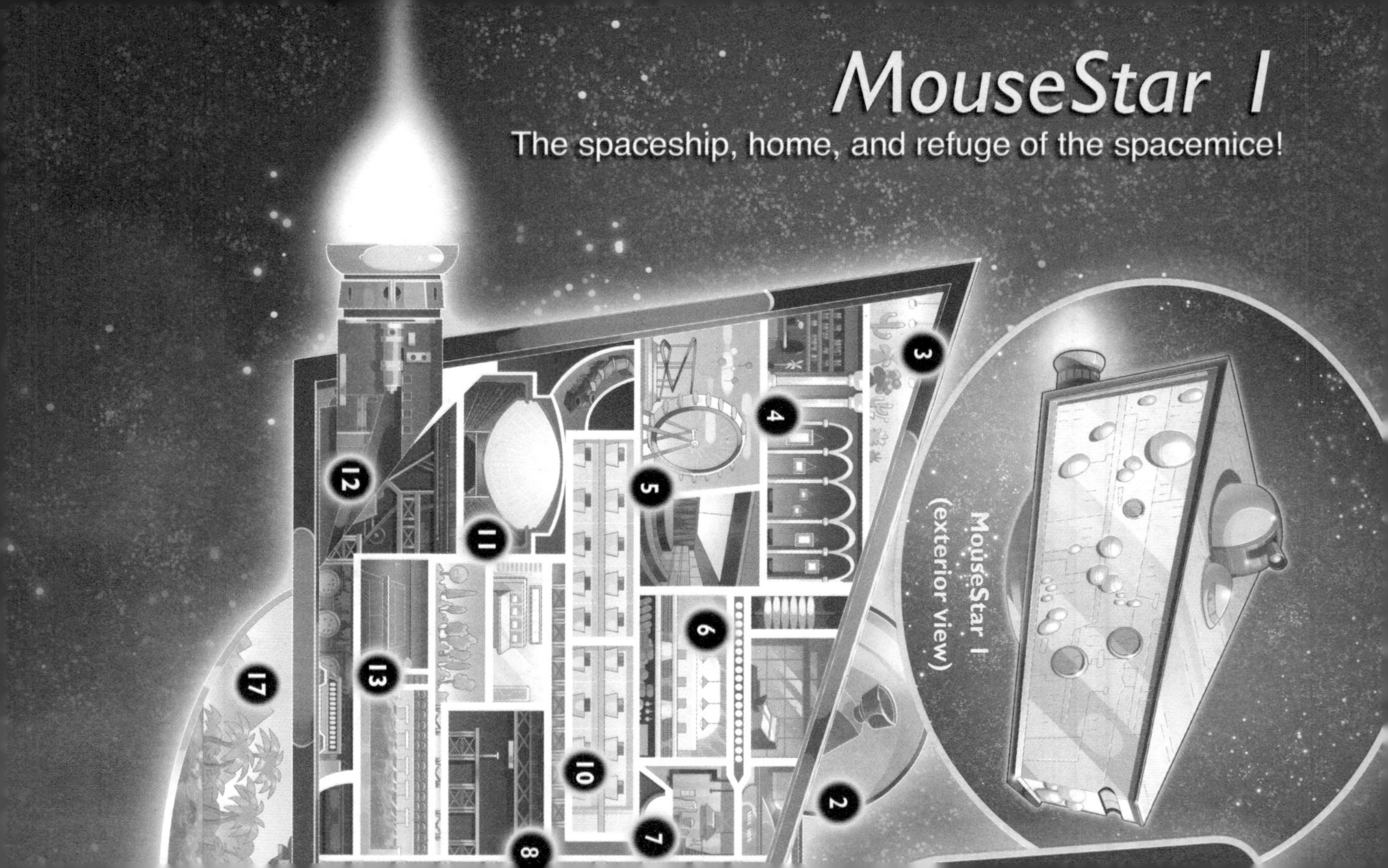
MouseStar 1
The spaceship, home, and refuge of the spacemice!
3
4
2
5
6
7
10
8
11
12
13
17
MouseStar 1
(exterior view)

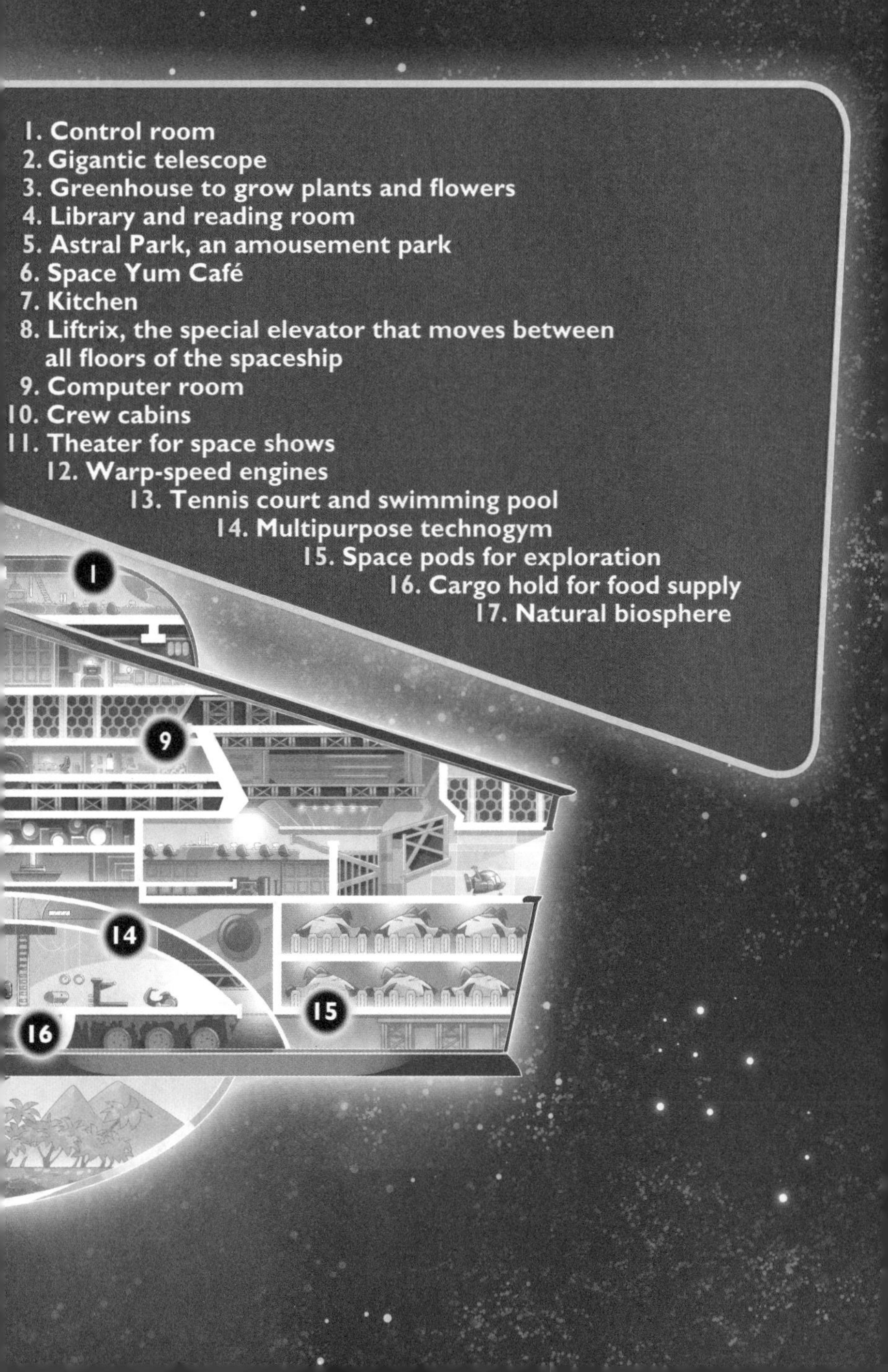
1. Control room
2. Gigantic telescope
3. Greenhouse to grow plants and flowers
4. Library and reading room
5. Astral Park, an amousement park
6. Space Yum Café
7. Kitchen
8. Liftrix, the special elevator that moves between all floors of the spaceship
9. Computer room
10. Crew cabins
11. Theater for space shows
12. Warp-speed engines
13. Tennis court and swimming pool
14. Multipurpose technogym
15. Space pods for exploration
16. Cargo hold for food supply
17. Natural biosphere
1
9
14
15
16

Dear mouse friends,
thanks for reading,
and good-bye until the next book.
See you in outer space!